THE SHADOW ON THE MOOR

THE
SHADOW ON THE MOOR

by
Alan Ian Percy
Eighth Duke of Northumberland

Ilustrated by
Liz Shallcross

THE SPREDDEN PRESS
STOCKSFIELD 1990

First published 1931
by William Blackwood & Sons Ltd.

© This edition published 1990 by
The Spredden Press
Brocksbushes Farm
Stocksfield
Northumberland NE45 7WB

© Introduction The Spredden Press

Printed and bound by
SMITH SETTLE
Ilkley Road, Otley, West Yorkshire LS21 3JP

INTRODUCTION

When Alan Ian Percy, Eighth Duke of Northumberland (1880-1930), died at the early age
of fifty he was described by one obituarist as
'Britain's Most Fearless and Outspoken Peer'.
He was the fourth of seven sons and had not
expected to inherit the huge responsibilities
that were to become his when his gifted eldest
brother, Henry Algernon, died unmarried in
1909, leaving him heir to the Dukedom. The
two brothers before him in the succession had
already died.

Before he succeeded to the title in 1918
most of his adult life had been spent as a professional soldier with the Grenadier Guards
in the South African War, with the Camel
Corps in Egypt, in the Sudan and in France
from 1914-16. He was also ADC to Lord
Grey in Canada from 1910-11 where he was
long remembered for walking from Montreal

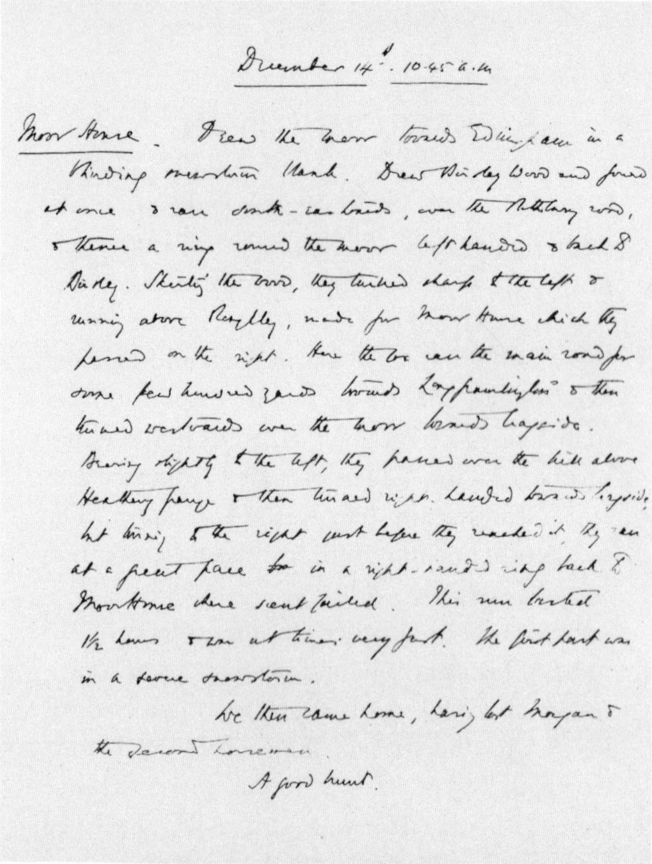

December 14th. 10.45 a.m

Moor House. Drew the moor towards Edlingham in a blinding snowstorm blank. Drew Birsley Wood and found at once & ran south-eastwards, over the Rothbury road, & thence a ring round the moor left handed & back to Birsley. Skirting the wood, they turned sharp to the left & running above Rugley, made for Moor House which they passed on the right. Here the fox ran the main road for some few hundred yards towards Longframlington & then turned westwards over the moor towards Wayside. Bearing slightly to the left, they passed over the hill above Heathery Fauld & then turned right handed towards Wayside, but turning to the right just before they reached it, they ran at a great pace in a right-handed ring back to Moor House where scent failed. This run lasted 1½ hours & was at times very fast. The first part was in a severe snowstorm.

We then came home, having lost Morgan & the second horseman.

A good hunt.

Extract from the Eighth Duke's hunting diary, December 14, 1928. Reprinted by kind permission of the Duke of Northumberland.

to Toronto in three days for a bet — in the middle of winter. After he became Duke he played a prominent part in public life as Lord Lieutenant of the County of Northumberland, alderman of Northumberland County Council and President of the Territorial Army Association. He was made President of the Royal Institution in 1919 and Chancellor of Durham University in 1928.

He was a leader of the right wing of the Conservative party in the 1920s and was regarded by some as a possible party leader held back by title more than anything else. As a gifted speaker and writer he felt compelled to proclaim what he saw as the dangers of Socialism and Bolshevism. His opinions were expressed forcefully and sometimes violently, and a series of articles on 'The Bolshevik Plot in England' which he contributed to the *Morning Post* resulted in a libel action against him from a Labour Party Member of Parliament. Yet the integrity and sincerity of his views won him universal respect, even from his political enemies. He was a popular landlord and a knowledgeable agriculturist.

Henry Algernon had distinguished himself in literature as well as politics, winning the Newdigate prize for English literature at Oxford and afterwards writing two books about his travel in Asiatic Turkey. Alan Ian wrote a large number of political and military articles and a collection of these were published as *The Writing on the Wall* under the pseudonym 'Daniel'. They were said to be 'remarkable for their accurate knowledge and logical deduction'. His two short stories, *The Shadow on the Moor* and *La Salamandre, the Story of a Vivandière,* the latter set in Belgium in the 1914-18 war, appeared after his death, in 1931 and 1934 respectively.

The Duke was a keen huntsman and *The Shadow on the Moor* is evidence of his love and knowledge of the Percy country as well as his power of dramatic description. Completed during his last illness it was published in the October 1930 issue of *Blackwood's Magazine.* It was subsequently published for private circulation by the Duchess of Northumberland but, because of public demand, copies were also made available to the public.

His greatest monument at Alnwick is probably the catalogues of the collections which he and the Duchess produced with professional help. The present guidebook to the Castle is based on the Guide written by the Eighth Duke and also published after his death in 1931.

The Shadow on the Moor.

AFTER twelve months on an office stool I had earned a holiday, which I spent fishing in the Border country. By good luck I found a spot as near perfect as anything in this world can be. The village inn was clean, the fare good enough, and the September weather gorgeous—in fact, too gorgeous for sport; but as I needed rest first and foremost, I was quite content to pass the day idling away the time, wandering up the burn or reading a book under a tree by its banks.

The burn was one of those which rise on the western flank of Cheviot, and it flowed for some miles through a narrow glen, the sides of which were in places almost precipitous, consisting of steep slopes of loose

whinstone, known in that country as
' glitters.'

The only persons I met in the course of
my rambles were a farmer, whose steading
lay at the lower end of the glen, about a
mile above the village where I was staying,
and his shepherd, a dour old man, whose
native reserve I never succeeded in pene-
trating. With the farmer, however, I was
soon on the friendliest terms. He was a
man of between sixty and seventy, of
some education though chiefly self-taught,
a great reader, and keenly interested in all
that was going on in the world, and a
story-teller of no mean capacity.

One evening towards the end of my
holiday I had stayed later than usual at
a pool which was swarming with trout
under Hauxley Glitters, the highest of all
the cliffs thereabouts. The sun had set,
and the mist was rising from the burn
so thick that one could not see more than
a few paces, when out of the mist there
suddenly loomed a man walking quickly
down the valley track. He did not see

me until he was almost at my side, and then started and drew back a little, but recovering, came slowly towards me, and I saw it was the shepherd. After exchanging greetings, he said, " I wouldna stop here after nightfall if I were you," and added, " It's no just very canny hereabouts when the sun is down." " All right," I answered, " I am coming," and, gathering up my rod and tackle, I accompanied him down the glen, thinking over his last remark, which aroused my curiosity. In the Highlands of Scotland I should have thought nothing of it, for the Celtic imagination has peopled that country with the figments of ancient paganism ; but the Border folk are of a different stamp, and I could not reconcile my companion's prosaic and rather grim personality with a belief in a visible spirit world. However, my efforts to ' draw ' him on the subject were unavailing, and I had to wait until I met the farmer, Jimmy Armstrong, next day, who, I hoped, would prove more communicative.

I was not disappointed. He laughed when I told him of the shepherd's remark. "Oh ay," he said, "old John wouldn't pass that spot alone in the dark for a hundred pounds. Not but what I myself would rather have company if I had to go that way on a dark night. But then, you see, I have heard the story from the only man who ever knew what really happened there. And, man, if you had heard it as I have, time and time again, from him who had it aye on his mind and couldn't shake it off, even on his deathbed, I'm thinking you would have a kind of horror of that place."

"What was the story?" I asked.

"I cannot tell you now," he said, "for I am taking some sheep to the mart, but if you'll look in for a bit of supper to-night, you shall hear it."

I duly looked in for supper, and when the meal was over and we had both lit our pipes, he began—

"Mind ye, I'm the only one that knows

the true story, for I had it from the lips, as I told you, of the only man who could tell it, because there was no one else present when the thing happened except my father, and he told it to none except, maybe, the rector. I think it was a kind of relief to him to tell me, who was the only son left to him, for in the last years of his life we were alone together, and you must understand that that experience was always like a burden on his soul for all it had happened so long before. I think he feared to speak of it to others lest they should doubt his story or even laugh at it, as maybe some had done long syne, and that was more than he could abide, for to him it was neither more nor less than making a mock of a manifest visitation of God.

My father was a lad of about twenty-two when it happened, and the date was 1827. This country was very different then to what it is now. The old gentry, who are nearly all gone now, had a grand time of it then: plenty of money they had, and they spent it too, what with the hunting, and the shooting, and the racing, and the cockfighting. The country houses were aye full in the winter-time for the sport, and most of them kept a town house at Chillingford as well for the dances and the parties and the Quarter Sessions. One of the best of the old squires was Mr Hollinshed of Reavely. He and his father before him had hunted this part of the country for fifty years, but at the time of my story he was too old to hunt hounds himself, and he had to find somebody to do it for him. He chose a man from over the Border, one Tom Fletcher, commonly called ' Black Tom ' or ' Gipsy Tom ' from his colour. There was some mystery about him, it seems : at least none knew how he was bred or where he came from. Folk said his mother was a gipsy woman who had died by the roadside when he was born, but who his father was nobody could say. He had whipped-in to one of the hill packs in Roxburghshire, I forget which, and he was a wonder with horses and hounds.

That was all old Mr Hollinshed cared
about ; ay, and it was all my father and
the other young lads cared about, too, but
there were some of the older ones who
shook their heads, for the truth is, Black
Tom, although he was the finest huntsman
ever breathed, had a character as black as
his face. Poaching had been his chief
employ in boyhood, that and fighting other
lads, to whom he was a terror, for though
not big he was made of steel, and desperate
quick on his feet. But there was worse
than that. At the age of fifteen he had
helped to rob the coach on Rimside Moor,
and only escaped prison on the plea that
he was the unwilling tool of a gang of
highwaymen. Later on he barely escaped
conviction for the murder of a gamekeeper,
and no sooner was that trouble over than
he was charged with horse-stealing, but
got off owing to some flaw in the evidence.
It may seem strange that such a lad ever
got into a hunting stable ; but this was a
wild country then, folk were not as par-
ticular in those days as they are now, and

he was worth his weight in gold when it came to breaking a horse or whipping-in to hounds. He had the temper of a fiend with his fellow-men, but the patience of Job with animals ; he could do anything with them, and they would do anything for him. It was said he had learnt to ride in a travelling circus as a child. His chance in life came when he was called on to hunt hounds in Roxburghshire for a few weeks owing to an accident to the huntsman. Then he became the talk of the countryside for the sport he showed. There was one hunt in which Black Tom killed his fox after hounds had been running five hours and covered thirty-five miles. He was riding a raw four-year-old that day which had hardly seen hounds before, but he swam it over the Tweed, though the river was coming down in flood, and jumped it over the park wall at Sunninghill—-a good five feet of mortared stone with a big ditch on the take-off side. After that nothing would content old Mr Hollinshed but he must have him to hunt

He jumped it over the park wall at Sunninghill

his hounds. Black Tom was by that time a man of maybe thirty or so. He had married about a year before, and by all accounts his wife led a dog's life; but the fact of his being married helped to persuade the Squire that he had settled down and was a reformed character. The man would have been good-looking in a kind of foreign gipsy fashion if it hadn't been that his nose had been knocked out of the straight and partly driven into his face in some fight he had had. He had curly black hair and short whiskers, and little dark eyes under great bushy eyebrows, very bright and always shifting about like a beast's. With his bullet head, square jaw, and broken nose he was a prize-fighter up above, and with his long legs and flat thighs a horseman below.

Whatever objections some folk may have had to Tom, they were silenced after he had been hunting the Squire's hounds for a month or two. Such sport had never been seen in this country before; and though nobody liked the man, they would

have put up with the devil himself for the
sake of the hunting. The chief trouble the
Squire had with him was that few men
could be got to serve him for long. With
the first whipper-in, it was true, he got on
well enough. Joe Sawyer was a middle-
aged hard-bitten man, and a master at
his job ; but the other hunt servants were
frightened out of their lives at him, and
were always giving notice or running away
without it, for the fact is that when Black
Tom was in one of his tempers there were
few more dangerous men on this earth.

The second whip, Jim Murray, was a
promising lad who put up with Tom, first,
because he knew that it was the best
training he could get, and secondly, because he had a wife and baby to consider,
though he was only a boy of twenty-two.
Jim got his chance of showing his mettle
not long after the regular hunting season
began, for Joe Sawyer fell ill, and he had
to take his place and whip-in to Tom.
And a hard time he had of it, so hard that
old Mr Hollinshed, who was a good kindly

soul, told Tom plainly he wouldn't have any lad in his kennels treated like a dog ; and after that there was no more cursing in public, but it's a question whether Jim didn't get even worse hell when there was no one to see or hear. What he must have put up with nobody knows, but he was a lad of spirit. He was learning his job from the finest huntsman if the worst man in England. He knew that if he stuck it for a few months he would make himself a name throughout the Border country, and he had not only himself to consider, but the wife and baby. Everybody liked him : he was always just where he was wanted, his voice was the best you ever heard, his view halloa had a peculiar wild kind of note that set your blood tingling, and altogether Tom and he made as fine a combination as you could have for hunting a pack of hounds.

All went well till past the New Year. Foxes were plentiful ; the season was open, and scent held day after day. Then there came a tragedy.

It was about eight o'clock of an evening towards the end of January. Dinner was over in Reavely Hall, and the Squire was sitting over his port in the dining-room with a party of friends, when the butler came in to say that the huntsman wanted to see him. Hounds had been out that day. Squire had been with them until early in the afternoon, and he thought Tom had called in, as the custom was, to tell him about the run.

'Good evening, Tom,' says Squire, 'have a glass of whisky. What sport have you had ? '

Tom never looked at him nor at the company. He walked up to the table, and he didn't seem to notice the glass which the butler held out to him. 'There's been an accident, sir,' he says ; ' Jim's had a fall on the road and broke his head.'

'Is he bad ? ' asks the Squire.

'Well, sir,' says Tom, 'I don't rightly know. He's unconscious. I stopped a cart which was passing and put him into it. They've taken him to the kennels, and I've sent a man for the doctor.' The kennels were only a quarter of a mile from the house.

' I'll come down at once,' says the Squire, rising. ' How did it happen ? '

All this time Tom was standing opposite the Squire, not looking at him but at the wall above his head. He didn't answer the question at once, but turned and took the glass out of the butler's hand, drained it dry, set it down, and wiped his lips before replying—

' It was by the turning to Benwick that it happened,' he said. ' Some hounds were lagging behind and I sent him back for them. I heard him trotting up behind ; then something must have happened— maybe his horse shied and threw him off. All I know is that it came galloping up beside me with no one on its back. I went back to see what had happened to him, and found him lying on the road. That's all I know.' Then for the first time—and it seemed as if it cost him a great effort — he looked Mr Hollinshed straight in the face.

The old man was really upset and wanted to go off there and then to the kennels, though it was a cold rainy night ; but the company all protested, told him he could do no good, and at last he consented to stay where he was and await the doctor's report. He came about an hour later, and gave no hope of Jim's recovery. His skull was fractured. How great the internal hæmorrhage was it was impossible to tell, but in any case his injuries were such as would probably cause death in a day or two. He proved to be right. It was then the Saturday night, and Jim died early on the Monday morning without, seemingly, having gained consciousness, though everything possible was done for him. Old Mrs Turnbull, the housekeeper at Reavely Hall, and the Squire's young daughter, Miss Anne, went to the cottage as soon as they got the news, and one or other of them stayed with Jenny, the wife, pretty well all the time till the end came, and the other neighbours gave all the help they could.

Jenny took it terrible bad. It wasn't only grief that seemed to weigh upon her, but a kind of horror and fright of something, nobody knew what. It wasn't till the Monday night that they could get her to go to bed. Mrs Brewis, the blacksmith's wife from Benwick, was with her that night, and one of the maids from the hall was minding the baby. Jenny slept a bit, and woke in the grey of the morning ; Mrs Brewis was asleep in a chair by the bedside. She awoke to find Jenny sitting up in bed and clutching her by the shoulder. Her eyes were blazing, her black hair was all tumbled about her face, and she was shaking all over with fear and excitement. ' Annie,' she says, ' I canna keep it to mysel' any longer. I maun tell somebody, and for the Lord's sake tell me what to do. Annie, do ye ken what Jim told me yesterday morning before he died ? ' Now Mrs Brewis knew, or thought she knew, that Jim had never re-

C

covered consciousness, so she paid no attention, and just tried to quiet her as you
might a child. But Jenny was not to be
put off. ' I've that on my mind,' she
says, ' that'll drive me mad if I dinna
tell it to somebody. I ken weel ye all
think that Jim never knew anything or
spoke a word after his fall, but I tell ye he
did—not only did he ken me but he spoke
to me. It was maybe a half-hour afore he
died. He gave a sigh, opened his eyes,
and looked at me steady-like for a while ;
then he says these words—he spoke low
but clear, and I could swear to them.
" Jenny," he says, " it was he that did it
—with his whip—' Ranter ' was left out—
I had miscounted the hounds—he was wild
when he knew it—and came for me." I
paid no heed to his words then ; I could
think of naething but that he was coming
round and would recover, and I told him
to lie still and not worry. He tried to say
something more, but it was just mumbling
and groaning, and soon after I noticed the
change in him and saw that he was going

She was sitting up in bed, quivering with passion

—you remember when I came out and told you. ' Annie, it was that man that killed him,' and she pointed in the direction of the huntsman's cottage, ' and, by God, he shall pay for it—a life for a life, say I.' She was sitting up in bed, quivering with passion, and shaking poor old Mrs Brewis by the shoulder. The old lady was a sensible canny kind of a body ; she didn't know whether the girl had imagined it or whether her story might be true, but true or false, it was clear to her that a hysterical distracted woman's account of what a husband with a fractured skull had said in his death agony was no kind of evidence, but she pretended to believe it, managed somehow to soothe Jenny, and at last got her to sleep.

As soon as Mrs Brewis had been relieved by one of the neighbours, off she goes to the rector with her story, and he, after advising her to keep her mouth shut, goes straight off to the doctor, who dismissed it as a malicious cock-and-bull story, as he called it, laughed at the idea of a man with such injuries being able to speak at all, and told the rector he would make short work of anyone who spread such a tale. That silenced the rector, but it didn't silence Mrs Brewis, nor the neighbours, especially as a rumour got about, spread, it was said, by one of the stable hands, that when Jim's horse got back to the stables on the night of the accident (if it was an accident), there was blood on the saddle. How came it there if his injuries were caused by a fall on the road?

For some days these rumours were flying abroad, and in the meantime Jim was buried in Benwick Churchyard. There was a great turn-out at the funeral, for he had been a favourite with all the hunting folk, and everyone was sorry for the wife and child. Jenny came to the funeral—very quiet she was, and never broke down once. Mrs Brewis kept with her all the time, and together they walked back to the kennels, stopping at the smithy for a cup of tea on the way.

When they reached the kennels it was

growing dark. The huntsman's cottage stood, as it stands to-day, on the right of the road, Jenny's a little farther on on the opposite side. As they passed his cottage, who should come out of it but Black Tom himself. He had been at the funeral, had just changed his clothes, and was going round to the kennels. He was only a few paces from them when he caught sight of them and made as if to go back, but Jenny put out her hand to stop him and went close up to him. Tom stood quite still with his eyes on the ground, and they stayed like that for what seemed to Mrs Brewis an age, though perhaps it was only a few seconds. Then Jenny speaks in a queer unnatural kind of a voice, very low and solemn, like a school child repeating a lesson. ' I kenned I wad meet ye,' she says, ' for I have a message for ye. I ken what happened on Saturday night. Jim told me——' Here Black Tom, for all he stood very stiff and still, gave a kind of shiver. ' Ay, he told me ; and now here's my message. My curse, the curse of the widow and the orphan, is upon you and shall remain with you until the day— and oh! it is not far distant—when you shall be called to answer for his blood. Till then no peace shall you have, sleeping or waking. Driven and hunted ye shall be—driven and hunted to your grave.

Tom waited till she had done, his eyes still on the ground; then he swallowed once or twice, took a deep breath, and turns to Mrs Brewis. ' Ma'am,' says he, ' you'd best take this woman home; she's mad and don't know what she's saying.' And with that he turned his back on them and walked quickly away. Jenny didn't seem to hear what he said. She kept on repeating the words ' driven and hunted, driven and hunted,' while Mrs Brewis dragged her off to her cottage.

All this was strange enough, but the strangest part was to come, for when Mrs Brewis got Jenny into the cottage she seemed to be in a sort of trance, sitting still in her chair with her hands clasped in her lap and gazing straight in front of her. All that evening she never moved or spoke, but at last Mrs Brewis got her to bed, and the next morning she seemed to be her usual self. But when Mrs Brewis said something about that meeting with Tom, what was her astonishment to find that Jenny remembered nothing about it, nor, which was queerer still, did she ever again refer to the manner of her husband's death, except once, and that was to the Squire.

That poor old gentleman was worried out of his life. Of course, the story had come to his ears, and he was furious that anybody should believe such things of his huntsman, and, still worse, bring discredit upon the hunt and himself by repeating them. Being the kindliest of men himself, the story was to him not merely incredible but utterly monstrous. Black Tom might have led a wild youth ; the Squire could well imagine a man of such hasty temper doing violence in hot blood—in a poaching affray, for instance—that was understandable and even pardonable ; but that one

man should attack another—and that other
a mere boy—in the dark on a lonely road
and deliberately beat out his brains with
a whip handle—and all for an offence
which was little more than a trivial piece
of negligence, almost excusable on a dark
night—that would be the act either of a
criminal lunatic or else an incarnate devil ;
and he could not bring himself to believe
that Tom was either the one or the other.
Still, though he didn't believe it, he had
never been easy in his mind since he had
engaged Tom. In his heart he disliked
and distrusted him. At times, it is true,
the dash, the reckless courage and amazing
skill of the man at his own game so carried
him away, as indeed it did all who saw
him hunting hounds, that it threw a kind
of glamour over him ; but at other times
he had a strange feeling that he was some
kind of evil animal, that his marvellous
power over animals was just due to the
fact that he had himself the nature of the
beast set in a human body—the cunning
of the beast, the fierceness of the beast,

the persistence of the beast, the uncontrollableness of the beast, combined with the intelligence but without the soul of a human being.

The Squire, in fact, was torn in two between his liking for Tom as a huntsman and his dislike of him as a man, but he was in no two minds as to the necessity for putting a stop to all the talk that was going on, and in this he was powerfully aided by the doctor. Between them they so frightened the folks with the terror of the law that they effectually silenced them. Jenny, however, still gave them some anxiety : it might be more difficult to silence her. Squire sent for her and told her he would give her a handsome pension and pay for the boy's education on one condition, that she never repeated her accusation against Tom. To his relief Jenny gladly consented, but the old man was somewhat staggered when she added, ' What for should I fash mysel' about him ? His account is settled, and he will pay it before the season's over.' This was said with such an assurance and in a manner so unlike herself, and as if she was speaking not her own words but some that had been put into her mouth, that Squire was all took aback and dismissed her without a word. The very next week he moved her to another cottage some miles away, for he could not bear the thought of her being in Tom's neighbourhood after that.

It so happened that the day after the funeral a hard frost set in, which lasted the best part of six weeks, and it was not until early in March that hunting could start again. Little was seen of Tom during that time. He seemed to avoid the neighbours, and it was said by the few who had seen him that he seemed changed, that he looked ill, and some said that he was drinking, though until then he had never been known to touch a drop. Indeed his temperance had been his only virtue. Whatever the truth of this may have been, he seemed to all appearance his old self when he turned up at the first meet after the frost ; and the only change that father

could see in him was in his manner of
riding. He had always been the boldest
of horsemen, but for all his dash he had
ridden with judgment and saved his horses
all he could. Now he seemed to have
grown not merely reckless but careless too,
not only of himself but of his mount. It
was almost as if the excitement of running
continual risks lightened in some way, or
made him for a time forget, some care
that weighed upon him. That something
was preying on his mind father was cer-
tain, and he had good opportunities for
judging, as he helped Joe Sawyer to whip
into him for the next few weeks. What
he particularly noticed was that the thing
which troubled him, whatever it was, seemed
to come more heavily upon him with the
fall of evening. He would get nervous and
anxious, almost as if he was scared of
something, and sometimes as father rode
behind him in the gathering dusk he would
see Tom looking back every minute over
his shoulder as if there was something
behind which he expected but feared to see.

His wild riding was noticed by all. He would take three or four falls every day, putting his horse at impossible places, and if this had gone on much longer there would not have been a sound horse in the stables. But it was not destined to go on, for fate intervened, as you shall hear.

On a day towards the end of March hounds met at the village of Helbury. It lies right away on the other side of the country close to the sea. It was blowing a gale from the east that morning, with cold sleet showers at intervals. There was not an atom of scent, foxes were all below ground, and covert after covert was drawn blank. There were not more than twenty people out. The Squire was not of the number, and his son, young Captain Hollinshed, who had just come home with his regiment from India, was acting master.

They drew northwards up the coast, and by about one o'clock the field had dwindled to half a dozen or so, all soaked to the skin and shivering, and so the Captain rides up to Tom, who was blowing

hounds out of Horwick Wood—it is a long
dene running down to the sea,—and says,
' I'm tired of this, Tom ; if we do find a
fox, hounds can't run in this gale. Take
the hounds home.' Tom didn't seem pleased
at the proposal. ' There's Cuthbertsborough whins, sir,' he said, ' it's a sure find ;
never known it fail yet, and I think the
wind's changing.' Captain Hollinshed turns
round to the few who were left and asks
them if they will go to the whins or go
home, and after some talk they decided in
favour of going on. There was the Benwick doctor, old Rattray, the two young
Weddells, sons of the farmer at Helbury,
Henderson the vet., Mr Ridley, the Squire
of Horwick, and his daughter, and another
farmer or two, and they all trotted off to
the whins.

It was and is still a grand covert, lying
close by the sea at the top of a long whinstone ridge which falls sixty feet sheer on
the inland side, and slopes gently down to
the sea on the other. That day, it is true,
the wind was blowing straight into it, but

there are so many clefts and hollows in
the rocks that a fox can find plenty of
shelter whatever quarter the wind is in.
It lies in the wildest part of all that coast
hard by the old ruined castle of Cuthbertsborough, as lonely and as beautiful a spot
as you'll find anywhere.

Tom was right about the wind. It did
change, and that so quickly that by the
time they had covered the distance to
Cuthbertsborough, only about a mile and
a half, it had veered round first to the
south and then into the west, and had
dropped to a mere breeze. At the same
time the clouds broke, the sun shone through
and dried their wet clothes, so that they
were all in better spirits by the time they
reached the whins, and were looking forward to a gallop. Joe went to the northern
end of the covert, and father and one of
the Weddell lads watched the west and
south sides. The rest of the field were on
the seaward slope of the hill.

They had not waited more than a few
minutes before there was a whimper. Then

one hound and presently another gave tongue, and there was no doubt that a fox was dodging about in the whins. " Huick, huick, huick ! " called Tom, and then he shouted ' Tally-ho ' as he viewed the fox across the open ride which ran down the middle of the covert, and father could see him pushing his unwilling horse through the prickly whins and jumping the bigger clumps to get to hounds. Still it was a slow business. The whins were thick, and the fox had no difficulty in avoiding hounds. At last they seemed to have lost touch with him altogether, and silence settled down.

As father waited there it struck him that there was something oppressive in that stillness. He used to say that, looking back on it afterwards, that queer sudden change in the weather and the quiet that followed it were the first of the many strange things that happened on that afternoon. It was all part of a series of events outside the ordinary course of nature, and from that hour everything seemed, at least as he looked back on it, unreal, as if it had happened on a stage set for some awful tragedy, in which he was compelled to play an unwilling part, and of which he was to be the only spectator.

Suddenly as he sat there on his mare he heard at the north-eastern end of the rocks a view halloa. He had been waiting for that sound, straining his ears for it, but now that it had come, he remained rooted to the spot, unable to move. For one brief moment it seemed so natural, so expected, so familiar; it was Jim's halloa. He had heard it a thousand times before. Then he remembered that Jim had been two months in his grave. He was so taken aback that it may have been some minutes before he pulled himself together, and, cursing himself for a fool, gathered up his reins, dug his heels into the mare, and galloped off to the sound. As he came out on the hill face he saw Tom not two hundred yards away standing still as a statue in the whins, his head up, as if listening intently. Father shouted to him that

someone was halloaing at the far end of
the covert, and at that Tom gave a jump
and seemed to come to himself, pulled his
horse together and followed him. As he
did so that halloa came again louder than
ever, ringing out on the still air, followed
by a long-drawn 'Go-o-one awa-a-ay
awa-a-ay,' and father said to himself,
'If that isn't Jim, then I swear it's his
ghost.' It had that same old ring in it
that his voice always had, ending on a
note that the finest singer might have
envied.

However, there were other things to
think of, and father soon gave up wonder-
ing whom that halloa came from, though
it just flashed across his mind that it
might have come from a shepherd whom
he had noticed standing on the rocks near
the place whence the sound had come, and
as he passed he shouted to ask which way
the fox had gone, but the man only shook
his head. At that moment father saw the
whole pack streaming out of covert below
the cliff and away up a thick-set fence

running due east, with the field a short
distance behind them.

He had got a bad start, and there was
no time to be lost if he was to catch them
up. He was riding a small blood mare,
not more than 15.3 hands high, and a
wonder over rough country. There were
two ways down the rocks : one by an easy
grass slope, but that meant going round
a few hundred yards out of the direct line ;
the other was only a sheep track winding
in and out among the boulders, and covered
with loose stones, but father put the mare
at it at a gallop, and she scrambled down
it like a cat. He had hardly reached the
bottom when Tom came rattling down
alongside of him with a loose rein, his eyes
set on the hounds and seeming to heed
nothing else, and the two rode on together.

Now to make you understand that run
I must tell you something about the country. There is a strip of rough grass-land
along the coast about a mile wide, with
dry-built stone walls and timber set on
top of stone-faced banks. As you go farther

Tom came rattling down alongside of him

inland you get into what was then mostly arable country some three or four miles wide. Then you come to rough grass again, and beyond that are the moors stretching right away to the Border, though there are cultivated valleys here and there. The great North Road runs along the edge of the hill country, which is generally about five to six miles from the sea.

For the first two miles it was a stern chase for father and Tom. The others had got a good start, and were a couple of fields ahead, but the pace was such that no one could live with hounds, and at one time it looked as if they would get clear away from everyone except Joe, who had been nearest to the corner where the fox broke, though he had not seen him. Tom and father were better mounted than anybody except the Captain, and they were not long in catching up with the field. Tom rode as if he didn't see the fences, and had he not been on the best horse in Squire's stables—a great raking chestnut with a grand turn of speed and an excep-

tionally bold jumper—he would have come
to grief at the first few fences, one of which
was a stout post and rails on a bank. Father
slowed up and the mare popped on and off,
but Tom went at it as if he was riding at
a steeplechase brook, and the chestnut had
to fly it. He just scraped over, hitting
the top rail hard, and this was a fair
sample of the way Tom took all his fences :
just touch and go every time.

They soon caught up and passed the
scattered members of the field. Old Mr
Ridley had pulled up, and was trotting off
home, leaving his daughter to go on alone ;
one of the Weddell lads was down ; and
Henderson, the vet., had lamed his horse
and was out of it. The rest were pounding
on as best they could far in the rear, all
except Joe Sawyer and the Captain, who
were riding close together with the pack
well in view. Father and Tom were gaining on them when hounds checked half-
way across a ploughed field. ' They've
flashed over it,' said Tom ; ' he's up that
fence to the right,' and he put his horse

at a great overgrown thorn hedge, crashed through it, and in another minute was calling hounds to him.

A cast back up the fence put them on the line again, but as luck would have it the next field was plough also, and carried no scent. Tom made a forward cast with no success, and the precious minutes were slipping by when from far away to their right front there came a halloa. It seemed to come from a little wood nearly half a mile away, and for all it was so distant father could have sworn it was the same voice that had halloaed the fox away from Cuthbertsborough Crags. The hounds heard it ; all their heads went up together, and they stood waiting for a word from Tom, but for a full three minutes he sat there listening intently while that voice rang ever more shrill upon the still air. At last the Captain rides up to him. ' It's all right, Tom,' he says, ' somebody's halloaing at Fleetmoor Strip.' ' Ay,' says Tom, without looking at him and as if he was speaking to himself, ' it's at Fleetmoor

Strip right enough, but who the devil is it ? ' The Captain was so taken aback at that that at first he could find no words to say ; then losing patience he raps out, ' And what the devil does it matter who it is, so long as the fox has gone that way ? ' With that Tom blows his horn and gallops off, followed by those three, and also by old Rattray, Miss Ridley, one of the Weddell lads, and two more farmers who had had time to join them.

They had not gone more than half-way towards the wood before hounds had got on the line of their fox, which had turned northwards. ' He'll be making for the quarry at Stonedyke,' says Joe to father, and indeed it looked like it. Stone-dyke is a little disused quarry with an old lime-kiln in it, a great refuge for foxes and difficult to stop. But as luck would have it, this fox ran straight past the quarry, and, turning inland, set his mask towards the hills. It was now about half-past two, one of those warm sunny afternoons you sometimes get in spring. The wind had fallen to a dead calm, hounds were running with a breast-high scent, two or three fields of heavy plough had been crossed, and horses were showing signs of distress. To make matters worse, the fox was heading straight up the long slope to the moors, a grilling task for a horse after five miles of heavy going. They had now left the arable country behind them and were riding over great rough grass fields which stretched upwards to the heather. Up this slope there was no living with hounds. They checked for perhaps a minute on the great North Road and then father saw their sterns flashing in the distance as they topped the wall on the far side and drove on westwards. From that moment they were lost to sight. It looked as if they would get clear away from everybody, and indeed by the time the road was reached there were only five in it—Captain Hollinshed, Tom, Joe Sawyer, Billy Weddell, and father. The rest of the horses were pounded, and couldn't even trot up the hill.

A convenient gate let them on to the road, but there was a fair-sized wall on the far side. The Captain went at it first. His horse knocked it half down and stumbled badly over the loose stones, recovering itself with difficulty, and the rest followed through the gap. West of the road the ground sloped gently down to a swampy strip with a ditch running through it, and beyond that it sloped upwards again to the hills. Up this far slope nearly a mile away hounds were racing, and as father took in the scene before him, the great bare country lying all bathed in the afternoon sunshine, the blue outlines of the hills, the pack straining up the slope in the distance, the faint clamour of their music borne on the still air, there came to him that feeling which comes to every sportsman who has the luck to be well mounted, when hounds have been going dead straight for half a dozen miles or more and the pace shows no signs of slackening—the feeling that he is in for a really good thing, an enjoyment which few will

The great bare country

share with him, one to be remembered all his life, but which will depend nevertheless on his own nerve and judgment, and a dash of luck into the bargain.

Galloping down the slope towards the boggy ground, the horses got their wind again. A high thorn fence patched with timber lay in front of them, and again the Captain's horse chanced it and nearly fell. ' He won't last much longer,' thinks father, and sure enough he flounders badly in the bog and pulls up with an over-reach. Father got through the bog first, being the lightest, and puts the mare at a stiff post and rails between it and the upland pasture which bordered the moor. As he did so he cursed himself for a fool, for there was a gate not fifty yards to his right, and it was an uphill greasy take-off and a bad landing ; but the mare checked, trotted up to the rail, got her hocks well under her, and took it with a good four inches to spare. Joe Sawyer came next ; his horse was blown and refused. Then comes Tom, who drove the chestnut at it in his usual fashion, smashed the stout oak into splinters, rolled over with his horse on top of him, but was up and mounted again in a second and galloping after them. Joe and Billy Weddell, thanking their stars, followed through the gap, but their horses were failing, and they found themselves falling farther and farther behind.

In this order they went on for another mile or more, passing a little lonely farmstead on the moor edge, where the goodwife, leaning on the garden gate with her hand shading her eyes, cried out that the fox had passed ten minutes ago very tired, and waved her arm to the westward. Hounds had disappeared once more over the edge of the hill, but as father and Tom came out on the hilltop they saw them nearer than they had dared to hope, barely a quarter of a mile away to their right front. They seemed to have checked and to be casting hither and thither, but even as they looked, Charmer and Remus picked up the line again, and they all went streaming away due west once more.

Father had eased the mare up the long slope to the moorland, but he now saw that if he was to get to hounds he must make a great call upon her. These moors carry a scent at all times, but on a day such as that, when you could hardly live with hounds in the low country, he knew that nothing would stop them on the hills. He took the mare by the head, gave her a touch of the heel, and she answered nobly, but still he could barely keep hounds in view. The distance between them and him was ever growing when the pack ran straight into a flock of sheep, and after a few minutes, during which they cast themselves every way without success, their heads went up, and they stood completely at a loss. Father galloped up to them with Tom at his heels. Straight on goes Tom with the hounds after him, but they can make nothing of it. Then he tries an all-round cast, still with no success, while father, who had dismounted to ease the mare, stands watching him. Suddenly something moving on some rocks to his right catches his eye. There against the sky he sees a fox sitting up on his haunches like a dog, looking straight at him. Father was on the point of waving to Tom to draw his attention when the animal gets up, shakes itself, and begins slowly walking up and down along the top of the rock, turning to look at the hounds every now and then ; and the strange thought came to him that the beast was trying to draw his attention, so deliberate were all its movements. He stood watching it until he saw Tom turning towards him, when he signalled to him, and as he came up he pointed to the fox, which was still doing sentry-go on the rock. Tom galloped towards the rock, with father bringing up the tail of the pack, and still the fox paces slowly up and down, just glancing at the hounds every now and then. Then when they were perhaps fifty yards away, as if judging that he had given them a sporting chance of catching him, he vanishes down the far side of the boulder.

Another half-hour followed with a screaming scent, and they had covered some four miles or more of terrible going, during which they caught fleeting glimpses of the hounds as they topped each successive rise, only to be lost to sight in the valleys. Then they came out on a high rocky ridge overlooking the valley of the Kimmer Burn, one of the tributaries of the Till, and the road to Chillingford, which runs up the valley. Below them were the pack once more at fault. On the other side of the valley lay the long slope of Banna Moor, and the great Banna Wood at the top of it. They clambered down the rocks to the hounds, scanning anxiously the farther side of the valley for any signs which might show which way the fox had gone, but there was nothing. The sheep were browsing quietly on the hillside. They shouted to a man who was fishing in the burn, but he shook his head. Evidently nothing had disturbed the peace of that valley. The fox must, therefore, have turned right or left or doubled back the way he had come. Tom swung down wind along the road to the right. They had gone maybe two hundred yards when he pulls up and sits staring with his jaw dropped. There, not fifty paces away on the other side of the little burn, stood a great dog fox looking steadily at them. As they gazed he trotted away a few paces, stopped, looked back at them, and trotted back again to the bank of the burn. It was absurd, it was incredible, but it came over father with the strength of a conviction nothing can shake that that fox was inviting them to hunt him. More-over, he was a fresh fox, and not the one he had seen on the rock a few miles farther back ; that one had been little and dark. Had this fox then been waiting for them ? Waiting—and for what ?   All sorts of strange wild fancies came into his mind. As he looked back on the circumstances of that afternoon it seemed that every-thing had been strange : the voice twice distinctly heard in the early part of the run, the extraordinary scent which lasted for miles at a stretch and then suddenly vanished, the strange behaviour of these two foxes as if they were intentionally luring them on. It seemed to him that there was some design in it all.

All this flashed through his mind vaguely enough, it is true, but it was sufficient to make him feel a little uneasy, and with his uneasiness came a feeling of anger at himself for these childish imaginations. He had not time to think it all out clearly, for hounds presently caught sight of the fox and were off like a flash. Tom and father did their utmost to stop them, for it was madness to start hunting a fresh fox ; but the attempt was hopeless, all the more so as the burn was unjumpable, with steep banks, and they had to look about for a place to ford it. By the time they had got across the pack were half-way towards the Banna Wood. That indeed gave them some comfort. It is a big wood, some two hundred acres in extent, full of great boulders, where a fox can get to ground in a hundred places. It was ten to one on their running him to ground even, if they did not catch him before he reached the wood.

In a few more minutes the pack disappeared in the wood, and father and Tom laboured up the rock-strewn slope a good half-mile behind them. Both horses by this time were tired and blowing hard, though they were still good for more if only the pace would slacken. They must have covered seventeen miles practically dead straight in the last two and a half hours, and at any other time father would have hugged himself at the thought of being in at the finish of such a run as that ; but as it was, his mind was filled with other thoughts. He wondered if all that had happened had seemed as queer to Tom as it did to him. Not a single word had Tom uttered during the last two hours, though they had been riding almost side by side. Father noticed now that he seemed to pay little attention to what was in front of him, but kept on turning round in his saddle and scanning the landscape behind him. Father looked in the

same direction. Far away on the other side
of the valley he saw a solitary horseman,
probably Sawyer ; that was the only sign
of life. One other thing he did notice,
however, but it might have been only
imagination : a patch of shadow on the
distant moorland, such as a cloud leaves
on a windy day, seemed to be moving
rapidly towards them. He gave it hardly
a thought ; it only struck him vaguely
as a little strange on such a cloudless and
windless evening. And then he dismissed
it from his mind as mere fancy.

As they entered the shade of the wood
his spirits fell still more. The westering
sun shone pink on the fir-tops far above
them, but down below it was dark and
still, oppressively still, he thought, as they
pulled up to listen ; but there was no sound,
save the panting of the horses and the
clinking of the bits.

'We'd better go different ways,' says
father. 'We'll have more chance of find-
ing them.' 'Not on your life,' raps out
Tom. 'You keep with me ; I shall want

E

you if we find hounds.' They rode on together, and father knew in his heart that Tom wanted him to stay with him for no other reason than for his company ; and that made him feel still more unhappy, for he had to confess to himself that he wanted to stay with Tom for precisely the same reason.

On the far side of the wood, to their intense relief, they came on the hounds. They seemed to be marking at a hole below a stone-faced bank. One or two hounds were scratching at it, but the others didn't seem too sure that the fox was there. ' Thank the Lord,' says father ; and he trotted off to bring the hounds back to Tom, who was blowing his horn for all he was worth. The pack showed a moment's indecision, but were just starting off towards him when a very strange thing happened.

A short distance away from where hounds had checked there stands an old ruined and deserted farmhouse with a few scattered stunted firs around it, known as Shepherd's Law. Round the corner of this building trotted a fox, which proceeded leisurely down the grass track towards them. At that a kind of desperation seized father. No fox should play that trick on them again, and he rode at it cracking his whip. The animal waited until he was no more than twenty paces away, then turned and ran. Immediately afterwards a piercing view halloa came from the far side of the ruined buildings. The pack instantly turned, and as the sound was repeated again and again — there was something strangely wild and thrilling in it—they tore along towards it.

Father might have made an effort to stop them if he had had his wits about him, but he sat there as if paralysed. Until that moment, as he often told me, it had never occurred to him to be afraid ; the worst he had felt was a kind of uncanny uneasy feeling. But now a wave of positive terror swept over him, such as he had not known since he was a little child lying in bed afraid of the dark; and indeed it was the same kind of fear. The voice was

the same that he had heard three hours
before—the voice of a man who had been
lying for weeks in the grave ; and as he
thought of it he felt his knees knocking
against his saddle-flaps, and a cold sweat
breaking out all over him. He fought
against his fear as a man in a heavy sea
fights to keep his head above the waves,
feeling that if once he allowed it to master
him he could never face his fellow-men
again. Mingled with his terror there was
shame and rage. What was there to be
frightened of ? All around lay the old
familiar landscape, the scattered patches
of whins, the brown bracken, the sheep
grazing on the hillside, the rabbits that
scuttled away into their holes in the bank ;
all bore a normal everyday aspect.

Then another wave of terror came over
him, for he realised that his mare shared it.
She was gazing in the direction of the buildings, snorting and edging away from them.
He could stand it no longer : he must see
what was on the other side of those ruins.
No power on earth could have made the

mare go up to them, so he circled round them at a distance, and came out on the ridge which looks down on the River Teamish. There was no sign of a human being. Below him hounds were in full cry. He could see the fox a few hundred yards in front of them making for the river. The startled sheep were running up towards him, and a flock of plover rose and circled slowly in the still air. For a moment he hesitated what to do. The road which led up the valley to his home not five miles away wound below him. Should he go home or go on ? Shame and, odd as it may seem, another feeling, curiosity, forbade. To leave Tom alone on those hills with night coming on, to get hounds home by himself, was in itself an act of meanness. What excuse could he make either to him or to others ? But besides this he felt he must solve the mystery which hung over the events of that afternoon. If unseen powers were really at work, he must discover what their purpose was. In fact, horribly frightened as he was, he felt he must go on.

Father caught it and brought it to Tom, who was still running
like a madman and looking behind him every moment

All this takes a long time to tell, but in reality it was no more than three or four minutes before he had pulled himself together and was galloping down the hill, and the sound of Tom's horse behind him confirmed his resolution to see the thing through. Tom at least was human flesh and blood.

The check, brief as it was, had done their horses good. There was a low stone wall between the moor and the riverside pasture, and the mare cocked her ears and flew it as if she was game for anything. Tom rode leaning low on the chestnut's neck, and looking round over his shoulder every minute or two, a gesture which puzzled father. He couldn't see the man's face clearly. He wore his cap very low over his eyes, and the collar of his coat was turned up as if he felt the cold, though what with the warmth of the day and the pace they had come father was sweating from every pore.

The river was big from the morning's rain. They forded it easily enough, but

there was a steep slippery bank on the far
side deep in mud where the cattle had come
down to drink. The mare scrambled half-
way up, sank up to her girth, and then
with a great effort pulled herself out. The
chestnut, however, stuck in the mud, slipped
back on the greasy slope, and fell over
sideways. Tom pulled himself out from
under the horse, and to father's amaze-
ment climbed the bank in desperate haste,
leaving his whip and his cap on the ground,
and began running in the direction the
hounds had gone. His horse, after getting
its breath, floundered up the bank, and
father caught it and brought it to Tom,
who was still running like a madman and
looking behind him every moment.

He paid no attention when father rode
up to him, but kept on running, and it
was not until father got in front and headed
him that he could make him stop. Then
in a kind of blind desperate hurry he
climbed panting into the saddle, and father
saw that the man was just mad with fear.
His cheeks were dead white, his lips were

dry, and great beads of sweat stood on his face. ' What is it ? ' says father. ' What's the matter with you ? ' ' Let go of the bridle,' says Tom fiercely ; ' for God's sake, let me get on.' But father still held the horse tight by the head, while Tom was urging him on with his heels ; there was a kind of struggle between them. ' I won't let go,' says father very steady, ' till you tell me what you're frightened of.' At that Tom seized his arm, the look of a hunted animal in his eyes. ' Look there,' he says, pointing behind them and licking his dry lips. ' Do you see that ? It's gaining on us ; for God's sake, let me get on.' He ended in a kind of wail. His fear was infectious, and father felt that awful terror sweeping over him again.

He let go of the horse and looked back. At first he saw nothing ; then he fancied he saw a shadow—it looked like a dark patch—sweeping across the sunlit tops of the firs in the Banna Wood and down the hillside by Shepherd's Law. Then he turned and followed Tom. As he rode on the

thought came to him that he was all alone
with a madman. Until then he had found
some comfort in the thought that he had
a companion. That comfort had been
taken from him. The fear that assailed
him had driven another man—and he the
most reckless dare-devil in all that country
—off his head. Would he go mad too?
It was useless to tell himself that he was
a prey to fancies and idle fears. Was Tom
a man likely to be influenced by such
things? No; they were both in the grip
of the powers of darkness, their sport and
plaything. Could a man conscious of that
hope to retain his reason?

He rode on blindly, mumbling little bits
of prayers to himself. Nothing else seemed
to be of any use in such a situation. But
all the time there was a fierce determina-
tion in his heart to see the thing through.
Whatever happened he was resolved that
he would lose neither his manhood nor his
reason, and the powers of hell should not
prevail against him.

You know the country they had now

reached. Hounds were running along those hills on the other side of this valley : they are grass, not heather, the going is good, but for the first mile up from the river it was all against the collar. The pace, however, had slackened considerably. Hounds hung on the scent, and now and then it looked as if they might catch them up. Every time, however, that they nearly did so, hounds would pick up the line again and drive on. Tom's horse could barely raise a trot in spite of the merciless way in which he was spurred : he rolled and blundered, and even the mare was showing acute signs of distress. It was evident that neither could last much longer.

They came out on the hilltop at last, and for a time the fresh evening breeze up there and the harder ground on the ridge enabled them to quicken their pace a little. Then the pack swung away from the river towards the western shoulder of Hawkhope. As they rode down the hill hounds checked in the bottom, and again they had almost reached them when clear

and shrill down the wind came that un-
earthly voice again. It might have been
half a mile away round the corner of the
hill to their right. Father's heart seemed
to stop beating for a minute ; then it
thumped so that he felt quite sick and
faint, and he had to hold on to the pommel
of his saddle. As for Tom, he was shaking
and quivering all over like a man in a
high fever. The sight of him was so
dreadful that father dared not look at him.

The valley in which they now were lay
in shadow. The sun was setting over the
hills to their right ; its long level rays still
lit up the upper slopes. The ascent from
that valley was an agony. Father had a
wild longing to get out of it and into the
sunlight above. The thought of the coming twilight added sensibly to his terrors,
yet it was no use to urge his mare on ; she
could only walk, and that slowly enough.
It seemed an age before they gained the
next ridge and turned their horses along
it. The sun was now full in their eyes,
dazzling them. They could see nothing,

but could hear sounds ahead of them running in the direction of the Glitters. With a great effort the horses broke into a jog-trot, the mare in front. Once father heard a sort of choking cry from Tom, and looking round he saw, or thought he saw, that strange shadow sweeping across the ridge they had just left.

The chestnut kept on stopping every now and then, and it required all Tom's frantic efforts to make it go on. All the time that he was spurring and whipping the poor beast, his head was slewed round over his shoulder to mark the advance of that nameless horror behind them. A sense of loathing filled father. What was the good, he thought, of staying with that creature any longer ? His face had lost all colour, the eyes protruded out of their sockets, the mouth hung open and dry and panting with the tongue out, exactly like a beast that is being hunted to death. If father was not to lose hounds altogether he must make a final call on the mare's remaining strength. He trotted on. There was another cry from Tom, but he paid no heed, and was soon out of sight of him round the shoulder of the hill.

The hill, as you know, runs out in the form of a promontory towards the Glitters. From the highest point to the Glitters is about three-quarters of a mile, a gentle slope all the way until you come within a short distance of the cliff. Then there is a steep pitch ending in the almost sheer descent of the Glitters. As he came round the shoulder of Hawkhope the long gentle slope lay before him. The sun was now on his left, and he could see clearly once more : that soft golden glow, which lasts for a few minutes only before the sun sets, lay over everything. The hounds, which were now heading straight up wind, were only a short distance in front of him, and had checked once more. Perhaps after all he might reach them and get them back to his own home before night came on. The thought that he was not more than three miles from home gave him some comfort. He hungered for the sight of his kind. The emptiness of those great moors, where, as luck would have it, there was not even a shepherd to be seen, filled him with a miserable sense of desolation. He was conscious also of a deadly weariness, physical as well as mental, and to add to his real fears there came all sorts of imaginary ones. Supposing the mare was to fail him; supposing he was benighted on those ghost-ridden fells. He put the thought from him—that way, he told himself, lay madness; but the thought would keep coming back in spite of everything.

The mare, feeling her head, turned towards home freshened up just a little. She was his only hope now, and in an access of almost childish gratitude he leant forward and patted and spoke to her. Then with a sinking heart he heard a hound speak, and they went on slowly working out the line until they vanished over the edge that slopes sharply down to the Glitters. When he reached the edge the steep slope below him lay in dark shadow, and at first he saw nothing. He

He caught sight of the hounds standing with their heads up at
the edge of the cliff

rode slowly on, looking about him for the hounds until he was only fifty yards or so from the Glitters. Then a little way off to his right he caught sight of the hounds standing with their heads up on the edge of the cliff. At last he would get to them.

He was turning in their direction when he heard the thunder of hoofs behind him, and a moment later Tom came galloping madly down the hill towards him. The chestnut was lurching and swaying : he had burst a blood-vessel, and the blood was pouring from his mouth and nostrils. The reins hung loose upon his neck, and Tom was looking behind him with one arm up like a man warding off a blow. Father tried to shout to him that the Glitters lay in front, but the sound died on his lips, for as Tom tore past him, something dark like a tall shadow seemed to sweep up from behind and to overtake him, and a scream like that of some hunted animal at the point of death burst from him. Father caught one glimpse of his face, and the eyes were fixed and glassy like those

of a corpse. But he saw no more, for as
that shadow swept past, the mare, mad
with terror, plunged violently and reared
up, hurling him backwards on to the
ground, and galloped away up the hill.

He fell flat on his back, and with such
force that all the wind was knocked out
of him, and for a minute or two he lay
there dazed and helpless, unable to move.
He remembered afterwards that it seemed
like an age while he lay there and listened
to the echoes of the crash as horse and
man rolled over and over into the depths,
and long after that sound had died away
he could hear the loosened stones slipping,
rumbling, and dropping into the water far
below. Then through the confusion of his
senses came that awful voice once more in
a long-drawn ear-piercing ' Who-o-whoop '
ringing up the chasm, the sound being
thrown backwards and forwards by the
rocks from one side to the other, until the
whole dark valley seemed to be filled with
exulting demons triumphing over a lost
soul.

That sound brought him to his senses, and he got up and ran back up the hill. He had only one aim, to get out of the shadow and on to the hilltop, where the sunlight yet lingered. As he came out on the brow he saw a man coming towards him leading his mare: it was Jimmy Anderson, our shepherd, the father of the Anderson who is my shepherd now. Father was so glad to see him and so unnerved by all he had gone through that he could only cling to him like a child. He couldn't speak; he felt that if he tried to do so he must have cried. Jimmy, of course, thought he had been knocked silly by his fall, so he took him by the arm and helped him down the path which leads down the north face of the hill.

When they got to the bottom father sits down on a rock and asks for a drink of whisky from his flask. Then he pulls himself together and tells what has happened. Jimmy thought he was wandering in the head, and paid little heed to his words, but they walked on until they came

round the shoulder of the hill and saw
the Glitters in front of them. There was
the horse lying in the middle of the stream,
and Tom's body a few yards from it on the
far bank. For a moment as they neared
it, father still clinging to Jimmy like a
frightened child, they thought the man was
alive, for the head was turned towards
them as if he had heard them coming.
When they reached it, however, they saw
that the body was just broken to pieces ;
but what daunted father was that the head
was still slewed round over the left shoulder
and the left arm was raised as if to ward
off a blow, in the exact attitude in which
he had last seen him, and the same stony
glare of terror lay in the wide-open eyes.
But that was the last straw ; father could
bear no more. ' Oh, cover it up,' he wailed ;
' for God's sake, cover it up.' Jimmy took
off his own coat and threw it over the dead
man's face, and together they walked on
to the farm. Father could never remember
how he got back here. His mind seemed
to have given way, and he was so worn out

A tall shadow seemed to sweep up from behind and to overtake
him and a scream like that of some hunted animal at the point
of death burst from him

that he couldn't walk without support. For some weeks he lay seriously ill. They feared his brain would be permanently affected, and indeed he was never the same man again.

And now you know why the folks in these parts won't go near the Glitters after dark."

" That's a very strange story," I said ; " but tell me, how do you explain it ? I mean the voice, the queer behaviour of the foxes, and the shadow ? "

" I can't explain it, and no more could father," he answered. " But he never doubted that Jenny's curse on Black Tom, that he should be driven and hunted to his grave, was fulfilled to the letter, and that on that day the foxes on the hills— ay, and the devils in hell too—were the ministers of a Divine vengeance."

I had nearly a mile to go to the village inn that night. It was very dark and still, and I have seldom enjoyed a walk less.